Praise for *I Feel Better Now*

"This lovely little book is a story of inner adventure. It uses timely circumstances to explore and explain timeless truths. Using the Covid affliction and its deeply negative effects on the physical, emotional and educational lives of children and teens, *I Feel Better Now* is a compelling literary device.

The book shows how, by changing our response to adverse situations through simple yet powerful techniques accessible to all children and teens, we can not only prevent outer turmoil from turning into inner chaos but also empower young people to discover that within each is a core of gratitude, contentment and joy."

Kate Fitzgerald, Owner Involution Yoga,
yoga instructor ERYT 500, board certified massage therapist

"Though it was created during the COVID pandemic, *I Feel Better Now* offers a glimpse into the emotional struggles kids are facing every day and offers coping strategies that can be used for a lifetime. Through her young characters, Hiba clearly illustrates the difficult emotions during uncertain times and validates the everyday struggles through her storytelling. Hiba is a talented Yoga and Mindfulness Teacher and her knowledge of these practices is evident as she guides her characters, Tommy and Alia, through several activities as a way to cope with stress all while exploring scenic Lewes, Delaware. The book transcends age and offers curative advice for all readers, especially children. I feel better now that *I Feel Better Now* will now be a new tool in the toolbox for parents, teachers and children."

Lisa D. Rector, Licensed Clinical Social Worker
Co-Founder of Minds Over Matter Initiative
Certified Mindfulness and Yoga Instructor

"Ms. Joy taught children valuable lessons but Alia encouraged Tommy to use these 'tools', right inside his own mind-body, to suddenly get stronger and . . . feel better. But without Ms. Joy's foundation and Alia's love, companionship, and timing . . . Who knows what might have happened? . . . I loved the book, the illustrations, the family connections, and the mindfulness tools. I loved all of it!"

Rachel Grier-Reynolds, L.C.S.W.
Board member of the Lewes Public Library

"After months of living with a pandemic, Tommy's big sister Alia leads him on a playful walk to the beach, away from feelings of loss and gloom and into the sunshine. In this beautifully illustrated story, yoga and mindfulness teacher Hiba Melhem Stancofski shows young readers and their families how to use the power of breath, awareness and simple movements to feel better right here, right now. What a gift!"

Beth Joselow, LPCMH
Executive Director of Minds Over Matter Initiative

I Feel
Better
Now

I Feel Better Now

About the Author:

Hiba Melhem Stancofski is a 200-hour certified yoga instructor, mindfulness teacher, and Reiki Level II healer in Lewes, Delaware. Her yoga trainings include vinyasa, yoga for cancer, yoga for trauma level 1, and restorative yoga. She is currently enrolled in a 300-hour yoga teacher training and will be 500YTT certified by late Spring 2021. She is a member of the Yoga Alliance and is a Mindful Schools-certified mindfulness educator.

Hiba has been teaching yoga for five years. She has taught at the Cancer Support Community, at yoga studios and gyms, at the Delaware Breast Cancer Coalition, and with a variety of private clients. She is also dedicated to introducing yoga to teenage athletes, teaching several athletic teams at the local public high school. Hiba is also part of Minds Over Matter Initiative and has taught mindfulness in schools in Sussex County, Delaware. This book is her first publication.

About the Illustrator:

Timothy Bada is an Illustrator/Graphic Designer from Lewes, Delaware. Timothy received his Bachelor Degree in Fine Art/Illustration from the School of Art and Design at East Carolina University.

From a very young age Timothy has been passionate about creating art. He has collaborated with artists of many backgrounds, such as musicians, sculptors, and writers. Working with such creative, lively people, molding ideas and exchanging critiques, allows him to push his boundaries in the creative arts.

I Feel Better Now

Written by Hiba Melhem Stancofski

Illustrated by Timothy Bada

This book is dedicated to
children and their caregivers
around the world. May you find
ease, may you feel safe and loved,
and may you feel better when
navigating life's hardships and
dealing with difficult emotions.

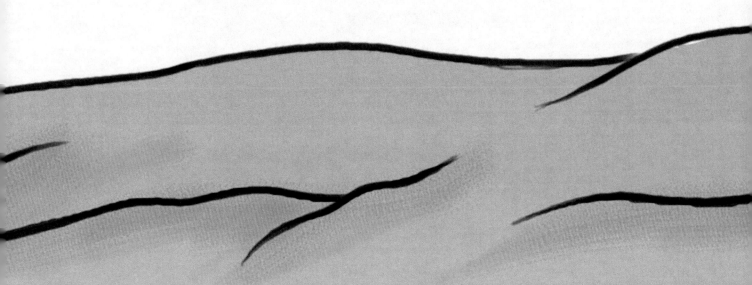

Tommy had been sad lately. Learning had switched to online classes and all activities had been canceled. He was home all day with his older sister Alia. He missed his routine, his school, and his friends. He missed his grandma too. She was sick and they were very close, but he wasn't allowed to go visit her.

Tommy didn't want to do anything. He just sat around all day, staring at the wall. He felt tired, even though he hadn't been doing much. He didn't like Zoom at all. Last week he'd fallen asleep during Zoom story time. He couldn't even hug Mrs. H., his favorite teacher, on Zoom!

He couldn't stop daydreaming about his favorite parts of school.

Things had been so rough on Tommy that he couldn't fall asleep most nights.

He couldn't stop thinking and worrying . . . tossing and turning . . .

4

for hours in bed, **wondering** when everything would go back to normal.

One morning, as Alia was walking down the hallway, she glanced into Tommy's bedroom and saw her brother. He looked sad, so small, almost invisible.

"What's wrong, Tommy?" Alia asked.

"Nothing," Tommy replied . . . "I'm just tired. Tired, sad, angry. Not sure which. I don't understand. Life is unfair. I miss my friends, sports, school . . . I even miss story time, Alia."

"I know, nothing is fair or right about this. Let's go out for a walk! Fresh air will do us both some good. Nothing like the sun to cheer us up."

"We'll walk into town, take a walk on the beach," said Alia. "I could use some cheering up, too. I miss my friends and activities just like you do... AND it's my senior year, you know!" she exclaimed. "Maybe we can practice some of the techniques that mindfulness teacher taught us at school to make us feel better. Do you remember that day? It was kind of different, but she said it would help when we feel stressed, sad, angry, lonely, or frustrated. It helps us deal with a lot of negative emotions when they get to be too much."

"Yeah," replied Tommy reluctantly. "I remember Ms. Joy and what she showed us. I've never practiced it, though. That stuff's stupid. Besides, I'd look ridiculous," he added.

"It's just you and me here, Tommy. Let's just pretend it's a game. I've actually been using some of Ms. Joy's activities before a game or test, and it does help! I can't just show you, though. You have to play along."

Tommy still looked unsure.

"Trust me, okay?
Maybe we can get ice-cream on the way back."

Tommy beamed and nodded.

"Cool," said Alia. "I'll go grab our masks, you go get our beach towels.
Let's go."

Alia and Tommy set off into town, and headed towards the church labyrinth. "Now as we're walking, notice how you're breathing," Alia began. "Not that it should be any specific way, but just pay attention. Is your breathing shallow or deep? Fast or slow? Smooth or choppy? Relaxed or tense? There's no right or wrong here. Just notice. Our breath can say a lot about how we feel."

After a moment, Alia added, "Breathe normally, walk normally. How many footsteps do you take while you breathe in? How many while you breathe out? Are they equal?" As they started walking the path together, Alia suggested, "Let your breath pace you. A rhythmic walk, Tommy, with your breath leading. Keep walking, follow your breath, and as you keep counting the steps, notice if either count changes."

"Let's add to this now," Alia said as they walked further into town. "I'm going to walk a certain way and you're going to mimic me and try to guess what I am. Ready?...... Who am I?" she asked.

"A robot!" he replied, mimicking her stiff movements.

"Who am I?" she asked.

A robber!" he exclaimed.

"Who am I?"

"The Hulk!" he shouted, following with a grunt.

"Who am I?" Alia asked.

"A dancer!" he replied as he did a clumsy pirouette, almost losing his balance.

"Let me try one," said Tommy. "Who am I?"

"A soldier! Sir, yes sir!" Alia giggled.

"Okay, let's keep going, and this time focus on your sense of smell. Give me 3 different smells you can sense as we are walking," Alia said as they walked across a drawbridge.

"Low tide! It's low tide. I can smell it, sis! Also, I can smell fuel from the boat engines. And..."

Ewww, did you fart, Alia? Gross!" Tommy's nose scrunched up.

"Yeah, no one's around but me and you! I can fart and burp all I want," Alia answered with a smirk.

"Alright, smart guy, how about 3 different sounds you can hear now?" Alia asked.

"I hear a boat engine sputtering, an ambulance siren further away... and seagulls cawing," Tommy answered after a brief pause.

Be Happy!

Alia and Tommy finally got to the beach. "Let's do some yoga postures now," Alia suggested. "Follow my cues, and don't overthink it. There's no right or wrong way to do it! We do these often to stretch before and after field hockey games. You move with your breath, like a breath dance." Tommy nodded. "Stand tall and proud, shoulders down, and gaze forward. Ground your feet in the sand. Steady, strong, and majestic, like a mountain. Now, breathe in softly, lift your arms up, reach your hands up to the sky, and look up. Don't you feel like you can touch the sky? Now breathe out fully and fold forward, touching the sand with your fingers if you can reach.

Let's do that four more times, moving with our breath. Maybe give me a smile as you reach up to the sky! Doesn't the sun make you smile?"

"Helloooo, sun!"
Tommy said playfully as he reached his hands up one more time.

"Now fold forward and pretend you're a ragdoll. Put your hands on opposite elbows and let the weight of your head hang heavy. Let's stay here for 10 breaths, just hanging here... Shake your head yes if you like this or no if I'm torturing you," giggled Alia.

"Let's try to be moons now. Take a full breath in, lift your arms up, palms together, and then lean to the left as you breathe out. Inhale back up to center, and lean to the right as you exhale again. Let's do that two more times in each direction. Remember, we're still moving with our breath. Our breath sets the rhythm of the movement. Can you lean deeper with each exhale? You look like a crescent moon!"

18

"Now pretend you're sitting in an invisible chair. Ground your feet down in the sand. Bend your knees. Keep your legs strong. Lift your arms and now press the palms of your hands together. Your gaze can follow your hands or you can gaze forward. Whatever feels right with your neck. Take five breaths here. How does that feel in your legs, your whole body? Let's play here. How low can you stay in your chair before falling on your butt?"

"My muscles are fired up, that's for sure! This isn't as easy as it sounds!" grunted Tommy.

"Okay, now lower into a squat and bring your hands together in front of your heart as if you're praying. Press your elbows into the inside of your knees. See how that helps you lift your chest? Now look forward. Why don't we see how long we can stay here? You know, before toilets existed, guess what? People had to squat just like this to poop! Can you imagine?" Alia laughed.

"Seriously? No toilet? No option to sit...ever?!" questioned Tommy in disbelief.

"Now take a deep breath in, open your mouth, stick your tongue out, and exhale loudly, forcefully. Like a lion."

Tommy stuck his tongue out.

"Not like a shy cat, Tommy! Give me a strong, loud sigh, get all your frustrations out, and make it forceful like a lion's roar. Now let's do that two more times while we're in this squat...AAAAAH!" Alia demonstrated.

"Alright, Tommy, now stand back up," said Alia. "Let's pretend we're trees. This is one of my favorites poses; on some days we're steady and strong, and on others we're wobbly and shaky. Place you right foot over the left knee, and press the palms of your hands together in front of your heart, or take your arms out like branches, swaying in the wind."

Tommy stumbled a little bit.

"It's okay to fall and try again," assured Alia. "Play, explore. We call it practice for a reason! Focus on the horizon. Breathe in, breathe out. Three more breaths here. Okay, now try your tree with the other leg Tommy. Notice if you're more balanced on this side. One side is usually more wobbly. Which one is it for you?!"

"Okay, now stand tall and steady like a mountain, hands together in front of your heart, and close your eyes. Think of one thing that you are thankful for today", directed Alia. "I know everything has been off or out of our control lately, but for now, just think of one thing that you are grateful for Tommy. It can be anything, from Mom tucking you in, to the sunshine, to Grandma's homemade cake, to playing soccer with Stan... Whatever makes you happy, little brother.

Even if things seem worrisome, there is always beauty in our lives. We just have to look harder on bad days. Look in your heart. What is one thing that makes you happy? Are you able to visualize that one thing with your eyes closed?"

Tommy thought hard about what he was grateful for.

"Now notice how thinking of that one thing makes you feel Tommy", Alia added.

"Okay, since we're on the beach and you love fishing, let's sit and try to be boats," Alia suggested. "Lean back a little, lift your legs, tighten your belly muscles, and keep your arms strong. Breathe in and out, gaze forward, and imagine you're a boat on the water, not rowing in a specific direction, but flowing wherever the current takes you. Visualize yourself going with the flow, rather than resisting it. Four more breaths here."

"Let's lay down for a few moments here. Your arms and legs are long, your palms facing the sky. Close your eyes and notice the sounds of the waves crashing on the shore. Pretend that we're wax sculptures, melting away into the earth with the sun shining bright on us. Breathe in deep, open your mouth, and sigh it out loud. Aaaah.... Now breathe in for.... 1, 2, 3, and breathe out for.... 1, 2, 3, 4. Again...."

Repeat quietly to yourself in your head 'I feel better. I feel better and better. Here. Now. I can rest.' Again, 'I feel better. I feel better and better. Here. Now. I can rest.'"

Tommy got quiet.

"Wake up, Tommy. You fell asleep!" Alia whispered after a while.

"I feel better, Alia, thank you. Can we lay here a little longer?" He turned towards her.

"We sure can. I'm glad you feel better. You know, things don't usually happen the way we expect them to in life. Things change constantly, and life often gets messy. It's okay not being okay all the time. When that happens, whether we're angry, sad, anxious, lonely, or are just having a bad day, these practices do help. They don't make our issues go away, but they help us deal with them a little more easily.

Who knows what tomorrow, next week, or next month will bring? No one knows. Maybe we can simply try to focus our energy and attention on ways to feel better today. We will deal with tomorrow when it comes. I hope our little walk helped with that. Of course, the more you practice, the easier it gets to feel better. Just like hockey or soccer, it takes practice."

Tommy nodded.

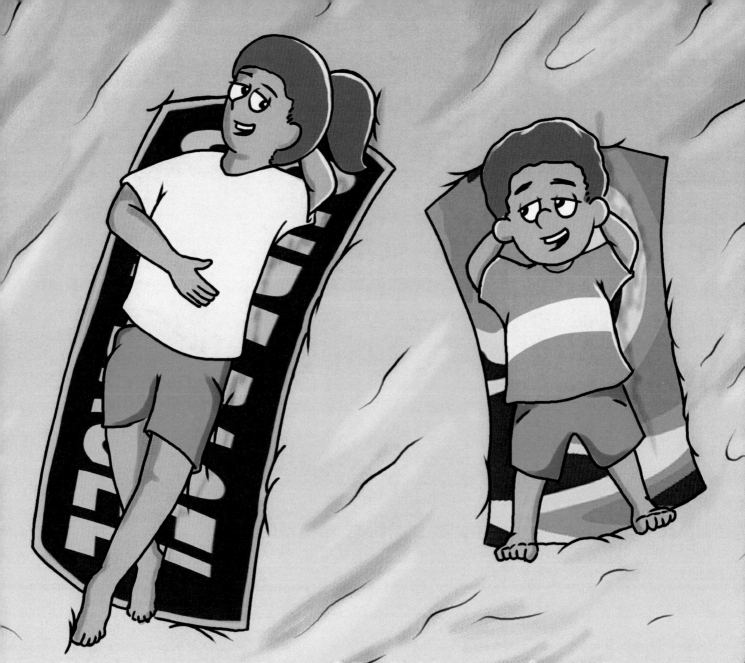

"And remember what Mom always says," Alia added, "we are here for each other, no judgment, only love. You could reach out to Mrs. H. Talking things out helps. Find your helper, and then find the courage to ask for help. The truth is, no one feels good all the time, not even on a good day. Most people just hide their feelings. I'm proud of you for telling me how you felt Tommy. Our emotions change constantly. We are never always feeling sad or always feeling happy. Right? So we have to be gentle with ourselves when our emotions get too intense."

Tommy smiled, feeling serene, and said, "You are my helper."

After a moment, Alia looked at him excitedly. "Hey, how about we go get that ice cream now?"

Tommy grinned. "Yes please!!"

As they walked out of the shop, cones in hand, Tommy looked at Alia with a smile. "This is one more thing I'm grateful for. Ice cream!"

"Me too, Tommy. Let's take our time to enjoy it!" she said with a chuckle.

28

ACKNOWLEDGEMENTS

I would like to thank all those that made this book possible; my husband Erik, for his unconditional support, my illustrator Timmy for his creative genius, and my three amazing children Romy, Erik-Stéphane, and Anna for their patient, positive criticism, and continuous editing and modeling input throughout the creative process.

A big thank you goes out to Beth Joselow (Minds Over Matter Initiative) for her unwavering support, and Crystal Heidel (Byzantium Sky Press), for her instrumental guidance and help publishing the book.

Other thanks go out to Kate Fitzgerald, Barbara Spears (Involution Yoga), and Andrea Kennedy (Yoga Studio on 24) for inspiring me, both as a student and as a teacher, each and every day.

"Everything will be okay as soon as you are okay with everything. And that's the only time everything will be okay."
Michael Singer, *The Untethered Soul.*

Discussion Questions for Parents/Caregivers

1. Have you ever done any of these activities before? How would you describe them? Easy, difficult, fun, weird? If you approached them with more curiosity and less judgment, do you think they'll get easier with practice?

- What was your favorite activity? Why?
- What was your least favorite activity? Why?

2. We tend to think and over think, and most times our thoughts are not positive ones. Sometimes we have so much going on in our head that everything becomes very overwhelming and unclear. Discuss how these activities, by focusing on our breath for instance, help us get out of our head.

- How challenging was it to stay focused on your breathing? Were your thoughts distracting you? What were you thinking? Would it be easier if you focused on your nostrils, feeling the air come in and out of them? Try again. Any change?

3. These activities are all about directing an intentional attention to our breath, our movement, or to each of our sensory systems, whether seeing, touching, smelling, tasting, or hearing.

- Which activity was hardest to stay focused on?
- How do you think being able to focus can help you in school? At home?

As Tommy focused to walk like a dancer, or a hulk, did you notice how differently he walked?

   • Do you think you would walk differently if you were happy or sad?

   • Does walking slowly make you notice more about how you are walking and how different parts of your body feel?

4. Have you ever noticed how your body feels when you are feeling strong emotions such as sadness, anger, or joy?

   • Describe how those emotions feel in your body. (For instance, when I am stressed, I feel the tension in my shoulders, or when I am scared, my heart starts racing).

   • Why is it important to notice these feelings? It is important because we feel our emotions in our body. By becoming aware of our thoughts and emotions, we can choose what to do with them. These mindfulness activities help us tune in to our body more, which in turn may help us notice our emotions more

   • How do you think that can help? Noticing how we feel can help because strong emotions can make us impulsive. Sometimes being impulsive, or "reacting" can be hurtful to others. For example, "I did not mean to hurt my sister's feelings. It just came out." Can you give an example of you reacting and saying something you later regretted to a loved one?

• Do you think it would be helpful to direct your attention to your breathing, for example, when you notice you are getting upset, before you even start reacting?

5. The mindfulness activities in the book, such as mindful breathing and mindful movement for instance, are some of the practices that help us find more clarity, focus, and equanimity in our mind, which in turn helps cultivate a healthier response to dealing with difficult emotions, and hence become better problem solvers when things get rough. By practicing mindful awareness of breath and movement, we are training the mind to respond differently.

• How did moving with your breath feel when you were practicing yoga postures? Was it difficult to stay focused and move in sync with your breath? Were you hard on yourself when you moved out of sync?

6. How did it make you feel to think of something you are grateful for? Use adjectives. It has been scientifically proven that a practice of gratitude improves brain function, makes us more hopeful and optimistic, and positively impacts our social interactions.

Made in United States
North Haven, CT
06 October 2021